AF380528

Clifford D. Simak

Time Hole

e-artnow 2020

Clifford D. Simak

Time Hole

Time Travel Stories by Clifford D. Simak: Project Mastodon, Second Childhood

e-artnow, 2020
Contact: info@e-artnow.org

ISBN 978-80-273-0895-8

Contents

Project Mastodon

CHAPTER I

The chief of protocol said, "Mr. Hudson of-ah-Mastodonia."

The secretary of state held out his hand. "I'm glad to see you, Mr. Hudson. I understand you've been here several times."

"That's right," said Hudson. "I had a hard time making your people believe I was in earnest."

"And are you, Mr. Hudson?"

"Believe me, sir, I would not try to fool you."

"And this Mastodonia," said the secretary, reaching down to tap the document upon the desk. "You will pardon me, but I've never heard of it."

"It's a new nation," Hudson explained, "but quite legitimate. We have a constitution, a democratic form of government, duly elected officials, and a code of laws. We are a free, peace-loving people and we are possessed of a vast amount of natural resources and —"

"Please tell me, sir," interrupted the secretary, "just where are you located?"

"Technically, you are our nearest neighbors."

"But that is ridiculous!" exploded Protocol.

"Not at all," insisted Hudson. "If you will give me a moment, Mr. Secretary, I have considerable evidence."

He brushed the fingers of Protocol off his sleeve and stepped forward to the desk, laying down the portfolio he carried.

"Go ahead, Mr. Hudson," said the secretary. "Why don't we all sit down and be comfortable while we talk this over?"

"You have my credentials, I see. Now here is a propos —"

"I have a document signed by a certain Wesley Adams."

"He's our first president," said Hudson. "Our George Washington, you might say."

"What is the purpose of this visit, Mr. Hudson?"

"We'd like to establish diplomatic relations. We think it would be to our mutual benefit. After all, we are a sister republic in perfect sympathy with your policies and aims. We'd like to negotiate trade agreements and we'd be grateful for some Point Four aid."

The secretary smiled. "Naturally. Who doesn't?"

"We're prepared to offer something in return," Hudson told him stiffly. "For one thing, we could offer sanctuary."

"Sanctuary!"

"I understand," said Hudson, "that in the present state of international tensions, a foolproof sanctuary is not something to be sneezed at."

The secretary turned stone cold. "I'm an extremely busy man."

Protocol took Hudson firmly by the arm. "Out you go."

General Leslie Bowers put in a call to State and got the secretary.

"I don't like to bother you, Herb," he said, "but there's something I want to check. Maybe you can help me."

"Glad to help you if I can."

"There's a fellow hanging around out here at the Pentagon, trying to get in to see me. Said I was the only one he'd talk to, but you know how it is."

"I certainly do."

"Name of Huston or Hudson or something like that."

"He was here just an hour or so ago," said the secretary. "Crackpot sort of fellow."

"He's gone now?"

"Yes. I don't think he'll be back."

"Did he say where you could reach him?"

"No, I don't believe he did."

"How did he strike you? I mean what kind of impression did you get of him?"

"I told you. A crackpot."

"I suppose he is. He said something to one of the colonels that got me worrying. Can't pass up anything, you know-not in the Dirty Tricks Department. Even if it's crackpot, these days you got to have a look at it."

"He offered sanctuary," said the secretary indignantly. "Can you imagine that!"

"He's been making the rounds, I guess," the general said. "He was over at AEC. Told them some sort of tale about knowing where there were vast uranium deposits. It was the AEC that told me he was heading your way."

"We get them all the time. Usually we can ease them out. This Hudson was just a little better than the most of them. He got in to see me."

"He told the colonel something about having a plan that would enable us to establish secret bases anywhere we wished, even in the territory of potential enemies. I know it sounds crazy...."

"Forget it, Les."

"You're probably right," said the general, "but this idea sends me. Can you imagine the look on their Iron Curtain faces?"

The scared little government clerk, darting conspiratorial glances all about him, brought the portfolio to the FBI.

"I found it in a bar down the street," he told the man who took him in tow. "Been going there for years. And I found this portfolio laying in the booth. I saw the man who must have left it there and I tried to find him later, but I couldn't."

"How do you know he left it there?"

"I just figured he did. He left the booth just as I came in and it was sort of dark in there and it took a minute to see this thing laying there. You see, I always take the same booth every day and Joe sees me come in and he brings me the usual and —"

"You saw this man leave the booth you usually sit in?"

"That's right."

"Then you saw the portfolio."

"Yes, sir."

"You tried to find the man, thinking it must have been his."

"That's exactly what I did."

"But by the time you went to look for him, he had disappeared."

"That's the way it was."

"Now tell me-why did you bring it here? Why didn't you turn it in to the management so the man could come back and claim it?"

"Well, sir, it was like this. I had a drink or two and I was wondering all the time what was in that portfolio. So finally I took a peek and —"

"And what you saw decided you to bring it here to us."

"That's right. I saw —"

"Don't tell me what you saw. Give me your name and address and don't say anything about this. You understand that we're grateful to you for thinking of us, but we'd rather you said nothing."

"Mum's the word," the little clerk assured him, full of vast importance.

The FBI phoned Dr. Ambrose Amberly, Smithsonian expert on paleontology.

"We've got something, Doctor, that we'd like you to have a look at. A lot of movie film."

"I'll be most happy to. I'll come down as soon as I get clear. End of the week, perhaps?"

"This is very urgent, Doctor. Damnest thing you ever saw. Big, shaggy elephants and tigers with teeth down to their necks. There's a beaver the size of a bear."

"Fakes," said Amberly, disgusted. "Clever gadgets. Camera angles."

"That's what we thought first, but there are no gadgets, no camera angles. This is the real McCoy."

"I'm on my way," the paleontologist said, hanging up.

Snide item in smug, smartaleck gossip column: Saucers are passé at the Pentagon. There's another mystery that's got the high brass very high.

CHAPTER II

President Wesley Adams and Secretary of State John Cooper sat glumly under a tree in the capital of Mastodonia and waited for the ambassador extraordinary to return.

"I tell you, Wes," said Cooper, who, under various pseudonyms, was also the secretaries of commerce, treasury and war, "this is a crazy thing we did. What if Chuck can't get back? They might throw him in jail or something might happen to the time unit or the helicopter. We should have gone along."

"We had to stay," Adams said. "You know what would happen to this camp and our supplies if we weren't around here to guard them."

"The only thing that's given us any trouble is that old mastodon. If he comes around again, I'm going to take a skillet and bang him in the brisket."

"That isn't the only reason, either," said President Adams, "and you know it. We can't go deserting this nation now that we've created it. We have to keep possession. Just planting a flag and saying it's ours wouldn't be enough. We might be called upon for proof that we've established residence. Something like the old homestead laws, you know."

"We'll establish residence sure enough," growled Secretary Cooper, "if something happens to that time unit or the helicopter."

"You think they'll do it, Johnny?"

"Who do what?"

"The United States. Do you think they'll recognize us?"

"Not if they know who we are."

"That's what I'm afraid of."

"Chuck will talk them into it. He can talk the skin right off a cat."

"Sometimes I think we're going at this wrong. Sure, Chuck's got the long-range view and I suppose it's best. But maybe what we ought to do is grab a good, fast profit and get out of here. We could take in hunting parties at ten thousand a head or maybe we could lease it to a movie company."

"We can do all that and do it legally and with full protection," Cooper told him, "if we can get ourselves recognized as a sovereign nation. If we negotiate a mutual defense pact, no one would dare get hostile because we could squawk to Uncle Sam."

"All you say is true," Adams agreed, "but there are going to be questions. It isn't just a matter of walking into Washington and getting recognition. They'll want to know about us, such as our population. What if Chuck has to tell them it's a total of three persons?"

Cooper shook his head. "He wouldn't answer that way, Wes. He'd duck the question or give them some diplomatic double-talk. After all, how can we be *sure* there are only three of us? We took over the whole continent, remember."

"You know well enough, Johnny, there are no other humans back here in North America. The farthest back any scientist will place the migrations from Asia is 30,000 years. They haven't got here yet."

"Maybe we should have done it differently," mused Cooper. "Maybe we should have included the whole world in our proclamation, not just the continent. That way, we could claim quite a population."

"It wouldn't have held water. Even as it is, we went a little further than precedent allows. The old explorers usually laid claim to certain watersheds. They'd find a river and lay claim to all the territory drained by the river. They didn't go grabbing off whole continents."

"That's because they were never sure of exactly what they had," said Cooper. "We are. We have what you might call the advantage of hindsight."

He leaned back against the tree and stared across the land. It was a pretty place, he thought- the rolling ridges covered by vast grazing areas and small groves, the forest-covered, ten-mile river valley. And everywhere one looked, the grazing herds of mastodon, giant bison and wild horses, with the less gregarious fauna scattered hit and miss.

Old Buster, the troublesome mastodon, a lone bull which had been probably run out of a herd by a younger rival, stood at the edge of a grove a quarter-mile away. He had his head down and was curling and uncurling his trunk in an aimless sort of way while he teetered slowly in a lazy-crazy fashion by lifting first one foot and then another.

The old cuss was lonely, Cooper told himself. That was why he hung around like a homeless dog-except that he was too big and awkward to have much pet-appeal and, more than likely, his temper was unstable.

The afternoon sun was pleasantly warm and the air, it seemed to Cooper, was the freshest he had ever smelled. It was, altogether, a very pleasant place, an Indian-summer sort of land, ideal for a Sunday picnic or a camping trip.

The breeze was just enough to float out from its flagstaff before the tent the national banner of Mastodonia —a red rampant mastodon upon a field of green.

"You know, Johnny," said Adams, "there's one thing that worries me a lot. If we're going to base our claim on precedent, we may be way off base. The old explorers always claimed their discoveries for their nations or their king, never for themselves."

"The principle was entirely different," Cooper told him. "Nobody ever did anything for himself in those days. Everyone was always under someone else's protection. The explorers either were financed by their governments or were sponsored by them or operated under a royal charter or a patent. With us, it's different. Ours is a private enterprise. You dreamed up the time unit and built it. The three of us chipped in to buy the helicopter. We've paid all of our expenses out of our own pockets. We never got a dime from anyone. What we found is ours."

"I hope you're right," said Adams uneasily.

Old Buster had moved out from the grove and was shuffling warily toward the camp. Adams picked up the rifle that lay across his knees.

"Wait," said Cooper sharply. "Maybe he's just bluffing. It would be a shame to plaster him; he's such a nice old guy."

Adams half raised the rifle.

"I'll give him three steps more," he announced. "I've had enough of him."

Suddenly a roar burst out of the air just above their heads. The two leaped to their feet.

"It's Chuck!" Cooper yelled. "He's back!"

The helicopter made a half-turn of the camp and came rapidly to Earth.

Trumpeting with terror, Old Buster was a dwindling dot far down the grassy ridge.

CHAPTER III

They built the nightly fires circling the camp to keep out the animals.

"It'll be the death of me yet," said Adams wearily, "cutting all this wood."

"We have to get to work on that stockade," Cooper said. "We've fooled around too long. Some night, fire or no fire, a herd of mastodon will come busting in here and if they ever hit the helicopter, we'll be dead ducks. It wouldn't take more than just five seconds to turn us into Robinson Crusoes of the Pleistocene."

"Well, now that this recognition thing has petered out on us," said Adams, "maybe we can get down to business."

"Trouble is," Cooper answered, "we spent about the last of our money on the chain saw to cut this wood and on Chuck's trip to Washington. To build a stockade, we need a tractor. We'd kill ourselves if we tried to rassle that many logs bare-handed."

"Maybe we could catch some of those horses running around out there."

"Have you ever broken a horse?"

"No, that's one thing I never tried."

"Me, either. How about you, Chuck?"

"Not me," said the ex-ambassador extraordinary bluntly.

Cooper squatted down beside the coals of the cooking fire and twirled the spit. Upon the spit were three grouse and half a dozen quail. The huge coffee pot was sending out a nose-tingling aroma. Biscuits were baking in the reflector.

"We've been here six weeks," he said, "and we're still living in a tent and cooking on an open fire. We better get busy and get something done."

"The stockade first," said Adams, "and that means a tractor."

"We could use the helicopter."

"Do you want to take the chance? That's our getaway. Once something happens to it...."

"I guess not," Cooper admitted, gulping.

"We could use some of that Point Four aid right now," commented Adams.

"They threw me out," said Hudson. "Everywhere I went, sooner or later they got around to throwing me out. They were real organized about it."

"Well, we tried," Adams said.

"And to top it off," added Hudson, "I had to go and lose all that film and now we'll have to waste our time taking more of it. Personally, I don't ever want to let another saber-tooth get that close to me while I hold the camera."

"You didn't have a thing to worry about," Adams objected. "Johnny was right there behind you with the gun."

"Yeah, with the muzzle about a foot from my head when he let go."

"I stopped him, didn't I?" demanded Cooper.

"With his head right in my lap."

"Maybe we won't have to take any more pictures," Adams suggested.

"We'll have to," Cooper said. "There are sportsmen up ahead who'd fork over ten thousand bucks easy for two weeks of hunting here. But before we could sell them on it, we'd have to show them movies. That scene with the saber-tooth would cinch it."

"If it didn't scare them off," Hudson pointed out. "The last few feet showed nothing but the inside of his throat."

Ex-ambassador Hudson looked unhappy. "I don't like the whole setup. As soon as we bring someone in, the news is sure to leak. And once the word gets out, there'll be guys lying in ambush for us-maybe even nations-scheming to steal the know-how, legally or violently. That's what scares me the most about those films I lost. Someone will find them and they may guess what it's all about, but I'm hoping they either won't believe it or can't manage to trace us."

"We could swear the hunting parties to secrecy," said Cooper.

"How could a sportsman keep still about the mounted head of a saber-tooth or a record piece of ivory?" And the same thing would apply to anyone we approached. Some university could raise dough to send a team of scientists back here and a movie company would cough up plenty to use this place as a location for a caveman epic. But it wouldn't be worth a thing to either of them if they couldn't tell about it.

"Now if we could have gotten recognition as a nation, we'd have been all set. We could make our own laws and regulations and be able to enforce them. We could bring in settlers and establish trade. We could exploit our natural resources. It would all be legal and aboveboard. We could tell who we were and where we were and what we had to offer."

"We aren't licked yet," said Adams. "There's a lot that we can do. Those river hills are covered with ginseng. We can each dig a dozen pounds a day. There's good money in the root."

"Ginseng root," Cooper said, "is peanuts. We need *big* money."

"Or we could trap," offered Adams. "The place is alive with beaver."

"Have you taken a good look at those beaver? They're about the size of a St. Bernard."

"All the better. Think how much just one pelt would bring."

"No dealer would believe that it was beaver. He'd think you were trying to pull a fast one on him. And there are only a few states that allow beaver to be trapped. To sell the pelts-even if you could-you'd have to take out licenses in each of those states."

"Those mastodon carry a lot of ivory," said Cooper. "And if we wanted to go north, we'd find mammoths that would carry even more...."

"And get socked into the jug for ivory smuggling?"

They sat, all three of them, staring at the fire, not finding anything to say.

The moaning complaint of a giant hunting cat came from somewhere up the river.

CHAPTER IV

Hudson lay in his sleeping bag, staring at the sky. It bothered him a lot. There was not one familiar constellation, not one star that he could name with any certainty. This juggling of the stars, he thought, emphasized more than anything else in this ancient land the vast gulf of years which lay between him and the Earth where he had been-or would be-born.

A hundred and fifty thousand years, Adams had said, give or take ten thousand. There just was no way to know. Later on, there might be. A measurement of the stars and a comparison with their positions in the twentieth century might be one way of doing it. But at the moment, any figure could be no more than a guess.

The time machine was not something that could be tested for calibration or performance. As a matter of fact, there *was* no way to test it. They had not been certain, he remembered, the first time they had used it, that it would really work. There had been no way to find out. When it worked, you knew it worked. And if it hadn't worked, there would have been no way of knowing beforehand that it wouldn't.

Adams had been sure, of course, but that had been because he had absolute reliance in the half-mathematical, half-philosophic concepts he had worked out-concepts that neither Hudson nor Cooper could come close to understanding.

That had always been the way it had been, even when they were kids, with Wes dreaming up the deals that he and Johnny carried out. Back in those days, too, they had used time travel in their play. Out in Johnny's back yard, they had rigged up a time machine out of a wonderful collection of salvaged junk —a wooden crate, an empty five-gallon paint pail, a battered coffee maker, a bunch of discarded copper tubing, a busted steering wheel and other odds and ends. In it, they had "traveled" back to Indian-before-the-white-man land and mammoth-land and dinosaur-land and the slaughter, he remembered, had been wonderfully appalling.

But, in reality, it had been much different. There was much more to it than gunning down the weird fauna that one found.

And they should have known there would be, for they had talked about it often.

He thought of the bull session back in university and the little, usually silent kid who sat quietly in the corner, a law-school student whose last name had been Pritchard.

And after sitting silently for some time, this Pritchard kid had spoken up: "If you guys ever do travel in time, you'll run up against more than you bargain for. I don't mean the climate or the terrain or the fauna, but the economics and the politics."

They all jeered at him, Hudson remembered, and then had gone on with their talk. And after a short while, the talk had turned to women, as it always did.

He wondered where that quiet man might be. Some day, Hudson told himself, I'll have to look him up and tell him he was right.

We did it wrong, he thought. There were so many other ways we might have done it, but we'd been so sure and greedy-greedy for the triumph and the glory-and now there was no easy way to collect.

On the verge of success, they could have sought out help, gone to some large industrial concern or an educational foundation or even to the government. Like historic explorers, they could have obtained subsidization and sponsorship. Then they would have had protection, funds to do a proper job and they need not have operated on their present shoestring-one beaten-up helicopter and one time unit. They could have had several and at least one standing by in the twentieth century as a rescue unit, should that be necessary.

But that would have meant a bargain, perhaps a very hard one, and sharing with someone who had contributed nothing but the money. And there was more than money in a thing like this-there were twenty years of dreams and a great idea and the dedication to that great idea-years of work and years of disappointment and an almost fanatical refusal to give up.

Even so, thought Hudson, they had figured well enough. There had been many chances to make blunders and they'd made relatively few. All they lacked, in the last analysis, was backing.

Take the helicopter, for example. It was the one satisfactory vehicle for time traveling. You had to get up in the air to clear whatever upheavals and subsidences there had been through geologic ages. The helicopter took you up and kept you clear and gave you a chance to pick a proper landing place. Travel without it and, granting you were lucky with land surfaces, you still might materialize in the heart of some great tree or end up in a swamp or the middle of a herd of startled, savage beasts. A plane would have done as well, but back in this world, you couldn't land a plane-or you couldn't be certain that you could. A helicopter, though, could land almost anywhere.

In the time-distance they had traveled, they almost certainly had been lucky, although one could not be entirely sure just how great a part of it was luck. Wes had felt that he had not been working as blindly as it sometimes might appear. He had calibrated the unit for jumps of 50,000 years. Finer calibration, he had said realistically, would have to wait for more developmental work.

Using the 50,000-year calibrations, they had figured it out. One jump (conceding that the calibration was correct) would have landed them at the end of the Wisconsin glacial period; two jumps, at its beginning. The third would set them down toward the end of the Sangamon Interglacial and apparently it had-give or take ten thousand years or so.

They had arrived at a time when the climate did not seem to vary greatly, either hot or cold. The flora was modern enough to give them a homelike feeling. The fauna, modern and Pleistocenic, overlapped. And the surface features were little altered from the twentieth century. The rivers ran along familiar paths, the hills and bluffs looked much the same. In this corner of the Earth, at least, 150,000 years had not changed things greatly.

Boyhood dreams, Hudson thought, were wondrous. It was not often that three men who had daydreamed in their youth could follow it out to its end. But they had and here they were.

Johnny was on watch, and it was Hudson's turn next, and he'd better get to sleep. He closed his eyes, then opened them again for another look at the unfamiliar stars. The east, he saw, was flushed with silver light. Soon the Moon would rise, which was good. A man could keep a better watch when the Moon was up.

He woke suddenly, snatched upright and into full awareness by the marrow-chilling clamor that slashed across the night. The very air seemed curdled by the savage racket and, for a moment, he sat numbed by it. Then, slowly, it seemed-his brain took the noise and separated it into two distinct but intermingled categories, the deadly screaming of a cat and the maddened trumpeting of a mastodon.

The Moon was up and the countryside was flooded by its light. Cooper, he saw, was out beyond the watchfires, standing there and watching, with his rifle ready. Adams was scrambling out of his sleeping bag, swearing softly to himself. The cooking fire had burned down to a bed of mottled coals, but the watchfires still were burning and the helicopter, parked within their circle, picked up the glint of flames.

"It's Buster," Adams told him angrily. "I'd know that bellowing of his anywhere. He's done nothing but parade up and down and bellow ever since we got here. And now he seems to have gone out and found himself a saber-tooth."

Hudson zipped down his sleeping bag, grabbed up his rifle and jumped to his feet, following Adams in a silent rush to where Cooper stood.

Cooper motioned at them. "Don't break it up. You'll never see the like of it again."

Adams brought his rifle up.

Cooper knocked the barrel down.

"You fool!" he shouted. "You want them turning on us?"

Two hundred yards away stood the mastodon and, on his back, the screeching saber-tooth. The great beast reared into the air and came down with a jolt, bucking to unseat the cat, flailing the air with his massive trunk. And as he bucked, the cat struck and struck again with his gleaming teeth, aiming for the spine.

Then the mastodon crashed head downward, as if to turn a somersault, rolled and was on his feet again, closer to them now than he had been before. The huge cat had sprung off.

For a moment, the two stood facing one another. Then the tiger charged, a flowing streak of motion in the moonlight. Buster wheeled away and the cat, leaping, hit his shoulder, clawed wildly and slid off. The mastodon whipped to the attack, tusks slashing, huge feet stamping. The cat, caught a glancing blow by one of the tusks, screamed and leaped up, to land in spread-eagle fashion upon Buster's head.

Maddened with pain and fright, blinded by the tiger's raking claws, the old mastodon ran-straight toward the camp. And as he ran, he grasped the cat in his trunk and tore him from his hold, lifted him high and threw him.

"Look out!" yelled Cooper and brought his rifle up and fired.

For an instant, Hudson saw it all as if it were a single scene, motionless, one frame snatched from a fantastic movie epic-the charging mastodon, with the tiger lifted and the sound track one great blast of bloodthirsty bedlam.

Then the scene dissolved in a blur of motion. He felt his rifle thud against his shoulder, knowing he had fired, but not hearing the explosion. And the mastodon was almost on top of him, bearing down like some mighty and remorseless engine of blind destruction.

He flung himself to one side and the giant brushed past him. Out of the tail of his eye, he saw the thrown saber-tooth crash to Earth within the circle of the watchfires.

He brought his rifle up again and caught the area behind Buster's ear within his sights. He pressed the trigger. The mastodon staggered, then regained his stride and went rushing on. He hit one of the watchfires dead center and went through it, scattering coals and burning brands.

Then there was a thud and the screeching clang of metal.

"Oh, no!" shouted Hudson.

Rushing forward, they stopped inside the circle of the fires.

The helicopter lay tilted at a crazy angle. One of its rotor blades was crumpled. Half across it, as if he might have fallen as he tried to bull his mad way over it, lay the mastodon.

Something crawled across the ground toward them, its spitting, snarling mouth gaping in the firelight, its back broken, hind legs trailing.

Calmly, without a word, Adams put a bullet into the head of the saber-tooth.

CHAPTER V

General Leslie Bowers rose from his chair and paced up and down the room. He stopped to bang the conference table with a knotted fist.

"You can't do it," he bawled at them. "You can't kill the project. I *know* there's something to it. We can't give it up!"

"But it's been ten years, General," said the secretary of the army. "If they were coming back, they'd be here by now."

The general stopped his pacing, stiffened. Who did that little civilian squirt think he was, talking to the military in that tone of voice!

"We know how you feel about it, General," said the chairman of the joint chiefs of staff. "I think we all recognize how deeply you're involved. You've blamed yourself all these years and there is no need of it. After all, there may be nothing to it."

"Sir," said the general, "I *know* there's something to it. I thought so at the time, even when no one else did. And what we've turned up since serves to bear me out. Let's take a look at these three men of ours. We knew almost nothing of them at the time, but we know them now. I've traced out their lives from the time that they were born until they disappeared-and I might add that, on the chance it might be all a hoax, we've searched for them for years and we've found no trace at all.

"I've talked with those who knew them and I've studied their scholastic and military records. I've arrived at the conclusion that if any three men could do it, they were the ones who could. Adams was the brains and the other two were the ones who carried out the things that he dreamed up. Cooper was a bulldog sort of man who could keep them going and it would be Hudson who would figure out the angles.

"And they knew the angles, gentlemen. They had it all doped out.

"What Hudson tried here in Washington is substantial proof of that. But even back in school, they were thinking of those angles. I talked some years ago to a lawyer in New York, name of Pritchard. He told me that even back in university, they talked of the economic and political problems that they might face if they ever cracked what they were working at.

"Wesley Adams was one of our brightest young scientific men. His record at the university and his war work bears that out. After the war, there were at least a dozen jobs he could have had. But he wasn't interested. And I'll tell you why he wasn't. He had something bigger-something he wanted to work on. So he and these two others went off by themselves —"

"You think he was working on a temporal —" the army secretary cut in.

"He was working on a time machine," roared the general. "I don't know about this 'temporal' business. Just plain 'time machine' is good enough for me."

"Let's calm down, General," said the JCS chairman, "After all, there's no need to shout."

The general nodded. "I'm sorry, sir. I get all worked up about this. I've spent the last ten years with it. As you say, I'm trying to make up for what I failed to do ten years ago. I should have talked to Hudson. I was busy, sure, but not that busy. It's an official state of mind that we're too busy to see anyone and I plead guilty on that score. And now that you're talking about closing the project —"

"It's costing us money," said the army secretary.

"And we have no direct evidence," pointed out the JCS chairman.

"I don't know what you want," snapped the general. "If there was any man alive who could crack time, that man was Wesley Adams. We found where he worked. We found the workshop and we talked to neighbors who said there was something funny going on and —"

"But ten years, General!" the army secretary protested.

"Hudson came here, bringing us the greatest discovery in all history, and we kicked him out. After that, do you expect them to come crawling back to us?"

"You think they went to someone else?"

"They wouldn't do that. They know what the thing they have found would mean. They wouldn't sell us out."

"Hudson came with a preposterous proposition," said the man from the state department.

"They had to protect themselves!" yelled the general. "If you had discovered a virgin planet with its natural resources intact, what would you do about it? Come trotting down here and hand it over to a government that's too 'busy' to recognize —"

"General!"

"Yes, sir," apologized the general tiredly. "I wish you gentlemen could see my view of it, how it all fits together. First there were the films and we have the word of a dozen competent paleontologists that it's impossible to fake anything as perfect as those films. But even granting that they could be, there are certain differences that no one would ever think of faking, because no one ever knew. Who, as an example, would put lynx tassels on the ears of a saber-tooth? Who would know that young mastodon were black?

"And the location. I wonder if you've forgotten that we tracked down the location of Adams' workshop from those films alone. They gave us clues so positive that we didn't even hesitate-we drove straight to the old deserted farm where Adams and his friends had worked. Don't you see how it all fits together?"

"I presume," the man from the state department said nastily, "that you even have an explanation as to why they chose that particular location."

"You thought you had me there," said the general, "but I have an answer. A good one. The southwestern corner of Wisconsin is a geologic curiosity. It was missed by all the glaciations. Why, we do not know. Whatever the reason, the glaciers came down on both sides of it and far to the south of it and left it standing there, a little island in a sea of ice.

"And another thing: Except for a time in the Triassic, that same area of Wisconsin has always been dry land. That and a few other spots are the only areas in North America which have not, time and time again, been covered by water. I don't think it necessary to point out the comfort it would be to an experimental traveler in time to be certain that, in almost any era he might hit, he'd have dry land beneath him."

The economics expert spoke up: "We've given this matter a lot of study and, while we do not feel ourselves competent to rule upon the possibility or impossibility of time travel, there are some observations I should like, at some time, to make."

"Go ahead right now," said the JCS chairman.

"We see one objection to the entire matter. One of the reasons, naturally, that we had some interest in it is that, if true, it would give us an entire new planet to exploit, perhaps more wisely than we've done in the past. But the thought occurs that any planet has only a certain grand total of natural resources. If we go into the past and exploit them, what effect will that have upon what is left of those resources for use in the present? Wouldn't we, in doing this, be robbing ourselves of our own heritage?"

"That contention," said the AEC chairman, "wouldn't hold true in every case. Quite the reverse, in fact. We know that there was, in some geologic ages in the past, a great deal more uranium than we have today. Go back far enough and you'd catch that uranium before it turned into lead. In southwestern Wisconsin, there is a lot of lead. Hudson told us he knew the location of vast uranium deposits and we thought he was a crackpot talking through his hat. If we'd known-let's be fair about this-if we had known and believed him about going back in time, we'd have snapped him up at once and all this would not have happened."

"It wouldn't hold true with forests, either," said the chairman of the JCS. "Or with pastures or with crops."

The economics expert was slightly flushed. "There is another thing," he said. "If we go back in time and colonize the land we find there, what would happen when that-well, let's call it retroactive-when that retroactive civilization reaches the beginning of our historic period? What will result from that cultural collision? Will our history change? Is what has happened false? Is all —"

"That's all poppycock!" the general shouted. "That and this other talk about using up resources. Whatever we did in the past-or are about to do-has been done already. I've lain awake nights, mister, thinking about all these things and there is no answer, believe me, except the one I give you. The question which faces us here is an immediate one. Do we give all this up or do we keep on watching that Wisconsin farm, waiting for them to come back? Do we keep on trying to find, independently, the process or formula or method that Adams found for traveling in time?"

"We've had no luck in our research so far, General," said the quiet physicist who sat at the table's end. "If you were not so sure and if the evidence were not so convincing that it had been done by Adams, I'd say flatly that it is impossible. We have no approach which holds any hope at all. What we've done so far, you might best describe as flounder. But if Adams turned the trick, it must be possible. There may be, as a matter of fact, more ways than one. We'd like to keep on trying."

"Not one word of blame has been put on you for your failure," the chairman told the physicist. "That you could do it seems to be more than can be humanly expected. If Adams did it —*if* he did, I say-it must have been simply that he blundered on an avenue of research no other man has thought of."

"You will recall," said the general, "that the research program, even from the first, was thought of strictly as a gamble. Our one hope was, and must remain, that they will return."

"It would have been so much simpler all around," the state department man said, "if Adams had patented his method."

The general raged at him. "And had it published, all neat and orderly, in the patent office records so that anyone who wanted it could look it up and have it?"

"We can be most sincerely thankful," said the chairman, "that he did not patent it."

CHAPTER VI

The helicopter would never fly again, but the time unit was intact.

Which didn't mean that it would work.

They held a powwow at their camp site. It had been, they decided, simpler to move the camp than to remove the body of Old Buster. So they had shifted at dawn, leaving the old mastodon still sprawled across the helicopter.

In a day or two, they knew, the great bones would be cleanly picked by the carrion birds, the lesser cats, the wolves and foxes and the little skulkers.

Getting the time unit out of the helicopter had been quite a chore, but they finally had managed and now Adams sat with it cradled in his lap.

"The worst of it," he told them, "is that I can't test it. There's no way to. You turn it on and it works or it doesn't work. You can't know till you try."

"That's something we can't help," Cooper replied. "The problem, seems to me, is how we're going to use it without the whirlybird."

"We have to figure out some way to get up in the air," said Adams. "We don't want to take the chance of going up into the twentieth century and arriving there about six feet underground."

"Common sense says that we should be higher here than up ahead," Hudson pointed out. "These hills have stood here since Jurassic times. They probably were a good deal higher then and have weathered down. That weathering still should be going on. So we should be higher here than in the twentieth century-not much, perhaps, but higher."

"Did anyone ever notice what the altimeter read?" asked Cooper.

"I don't believe I did," Adams admitted.

"It wouldn't tell you, anyhow," Hudson declared. "It would just give our height then and now-and we were moving, remember-and what about air pockets and relative atmosphere density and all the rest?"

Cooper looked as discouraged as Hudson felt.

"How does this sound?" asked Adams. "We'll build a platform twelve feet high. That certainly should be enough to clear us and yet small enough to stay within the range of the unit's force-field."

"And what if we're two feet higher here?" Hudson pointed out.

"A fall of fourteen feet wouldn't kill a man unless he's plain unlucky."

"It might break some bones."

"So it might break some bones. You want to stay here or take a chance on a broken leg?"

"All right, if you put it that way. A platform, you say. A platform out of what?"

"Timber. There's lot of it. We just go out and cut some logs."

"A twelve-foot log is heavy. And how are we going to get that big a log uphill?"

"We drag it."

"We try to, you mean."

"Maybe we could fix up a cart," said Adams, after thinking a moment.

"Out of what?" Cooper asked.

"Rollers, maybe. We could cut some and roll the logs up here."

"That would work on level ground," Hudson said. "It wouldn't work to roll a log uphill. It would get away from us. Someone might get killed."

"The logs would have to be longer than twelve feet, anyhow," Cooper put in. "You'd have to set them in a hole and that takes away some footage."

"Why not the tripod principle?" Hudson offered. "Fasten three logs at the top and raise them."

"That's a gin-pole, a primitive derrick. It'd still have to be longer than twelve feet. Fifteen, sixteen, maybe. And how are we going to hoist three sixteen-foot logs? We'd need a block and tackle."

"There's another thing," said Cooper. "Part of those logs might just be beyond the effective range of the force-field. Part of them would have to —*have to*, mind you-move in time and part couldn't. That would set up a stress...."

"Another thing about it," added Hudson, "is that we'd travel with the logs. I don't want to come out in another time with a bunch of logs flying all around me."

"Cheer up," Adams told them. "Maybe the unit won't work, anyhow."

CHAPTER VII

The general sat alone in his office and held his head between his hands. The fools, he thought, the goddam knuckle-headed fools! Why couldn't they see it as clearly as he did?

For fifteen years now, as head of Project Mastodon, he had lived with it night and day and he could see all the possibilities as clearly as if they had been actual fact. Not military possibilities alone, although as a military man, he naturally would think of those first.

The hidden bases, for example, located within the very strongholds of potential enemies-within, yet centuries removed in time. Many centuries removed and only seconds distant.

He could see it all: The materialization of the fleets; the swift, devastating blow, then the instantaneous retreat into the fastnesses of the past. Terrific destruction, but not a ship lost nor a man.

Except that if you had the bases, you need never strike the blow. If you had the bases and let the enemy know you had them, there would never be the provocation.

And on the home front, you'd have air-raid shelters that would be effective. You'd evacuate your population not in space, but time. You'd have the sure and absolute defense against any kind of bombing-fission, fusion, bacteriological or whatever else the labs had in stock.

And if the worst should come-which it never would with a setup like that-you'd have a place to which the entire nation could retreat, leaving to the enemy the empty, blasted cities and the lethally dusted countryside.

Sanctuary-that had been what Hudson had offered the then-secretary of state fifteen years ago-and the idiot had frozen up with the insult of it and had Hudson thrown out.

And if war did not come, think of the living space and the vast new opportunities-not the least of which would be the opportunity to achieve peaceful living in a virgin world, where the old hatreds would slough off and new concepts have a chance to grow.

He wondered where they were, those three who had gone back into time. Dead, perhaps. Run down by a mastodon. Or stalked by tigers. Or maybe done in by warlike tribesmen. No, he kept forgetting there weren't any in that era. Or trapped in time, unable to get back, condemned to exile in an alien time. Or maybe, he thought, just plain disgusted. And he couldn't blame them if they were.

Or maybe-let's be fantastic about this-sneaking in colonists from some place other than the watched Wisconsin farm, building up in actuality the nation they had claimed to be.

They had to get back to the present soon or Project Mastodon would be killed entirely. Already the research program had been halted and if something didn't happen quickly, the watch that was kept on the Wisconsin farm would be called off.

"And if they do that," said the general, "I know just what I'll do."

He got up and strode around the room.

"By God," he said, "I'll show 'em!"

CHAPTER VIII

It had taken ten full days of back-breaking work to build the pyramid. They'd hauled the rocks from the creek bed half a mile away and had piled them, stone by rolling stone, to the height of a full twelve feet. It took a lot of rocks and a lot of patience, for as the pyramid went up, the base naturally kept broadening out.

But now all was finally ready.

Hudson sat before the burned-out campfire and held his blistered hands before him.

It should work, he thought, better than the logs-and less dangerous.

Grab a handful of sand. Some trickled back between your fingers, but most stayed in your grasp. That was the principle of the pyramid of stones. When-and if-the time machine should work, most of the rocks would go along.

Those that didn't go would simply trickle out and do no harm. There'd be no stress or strain to upset the working of the force-field.

And if the time unit didn't work?

Or if it did?

This was the end of the dream, thought Hudson, no matter how you looked at it.

For even if they did get back to the twentieth century, there would be no money and with the film lost and no other taken to replace it, they'd have no proof they had traveled back beyond the dawn of history-back almost to the dawn of Man.

Although how far you traveled would have no significance. An hour or a million years would be all the same; if you could span the hour, you could span the million years. And if you could go back the million years, it was within your power to go back to the first tick of eternity, the first stir of time across the face of emptiness and nothingness-back to that initial instant when nothing as yet had happened or been planned or thought, when all the vastness of the Universe was a new slate waiting the first chalk stroke of destiny.

Another helicopter would cost thirty thousand dollars-and they didn't even have the money to buy the tractor that they needed to build the stockade.

There was no way to borrow. You couldn't walk into a bank and say you wanted thirty thousand to take a trip back to the Old Stone Age.

You still could go to some industry or some university or the government and if you could persuade them you had something on the ball-why, then, they might put up the cash after cutting themselves in on just about all of the profits. And, naturally, they'd run the show because it was their money and all you had done was the sweating and the bleeding.

"There's one thing that still bothers me," said Cooper, breaking the silence. "We spent a lot of time picking our spot so we'd miss the barn and house and all the other buildings...."

"Don't tell me the windmill!" Hudson cried.

"No. I'm pretty sure we're clear of that. But the way I figure, we're right astraddle that barbed-wire fence at the south end of the orchard."

"If you want, we could move the pyramid over twenty feet or so."

Cooper groaned. "I'll take my chances with the fence." Adams got to his feet, the time unit tucked underneath his arm. "Come on, you guys. It's time to go."

They climbed the pyramid gingerly and stood unsteadily at its top.

Adams shifted the unit around, clasped it to his chest.

"Stand around close," he said, "and bend your knees a little. It may be quite a drop."

"Go ahead," said Cooper. "Press the button."

Adams pressed the button.

Nothing happened.

The unit didn't work.

CHAPTER IX

The chief of Central Intelligence was white-lipped when he finished talking.

"You're sure of your information?" asked the President.

"Mr. President," said the CIA chief, "I've never been more sure of anything in my entire life."

The President looked at the other two who were in the room, a question in his eyes.

The JCS chairman said, "It checks, sir, with everything we know."

"But it's incredible!" the President said.

"They're afraid," said the CIA chief. "They lie awake nights. They've become convinced that we're on the verge of traveling in time. They've tried and failed, but they think we're near success. To their way of thinking, they've got to hit us now or never, because once we actually get time travel, they know their number's up."

"But we dropped Project Mastodon entirely almost three years ago. It's been all of ten years since we stopped the research. It was twenty-five years ago that Hudson —"

"That makes no difference, sir. They're convinced we dropped the project publicly, but went underground with it. That would be the kind of strategy they could understand."

The President picked up a pencil and doodled on a pad.

"Who was that old general," he asked, "the one who raised so much fuss when we dropped the project? I remember I was in the Senate then. He came around to see me."

"Bowers, sir," said the JCS chairman.

"That's right. What became of him?"

"Retired."

"Well, I guess it doesn't make any difference now." He doodled some more and finally said, "Gentlemen, it looks like this is it. How much time did you say we had?"

"Not more than ninety days, sir. Maybe as little as thirty."

The President looked up at the JCS chairman.

"We're as ready," said the chairman, "as we will ever be. We can handle them —I think. There will, of course, be some —"

"I know," said the President.

"Could we bluff?" asked the secretary of state, speaking quietly. "I know it wouldn't stick, but at least we might buy some time."

"You mean hint that we have time travel?"

The secretary nodded.

"It wouldn't work," said the CIA chief tiredly. "If we really had it, there'd be no question then. They'd become exceedingly well-mannered, even neighborly, if they were sure we had it."

"But we haven't got it," said the President gloomily.

CHAPTER X

The two hunters trudged homeward late in the afternoon, with a deer slung from a pole they carried on their shoulders. Their breath hung visibly in the air as they walked along, for the frost had come and any day now, they knew, there would be snow.

"I'm worried about Wes," said Cooper, breathing heavily. "He's taking this too hard. We got to keep an eye on him."

"Let's take a rest," panted Hudson.

They halted and lowered the deer to the ground.

"He blames himself too much," said Cooper. He wiped his sweaty forehead. "There isn't any need to. All of us walked into this with our eyes wide open."

"He's kidding himself and he knows it, but it gives him something to go on. As long as he can keep busy with all his puttering around, he'll be all right."

"He isn't going to repair the time unit, Chuck."

"I know he isn't. And he knows it, too. He hasn't got the tools or the materials. Back in the workshop, he might have a chance, but here he hasn't."

"It's rough on him."

"It's rough on all of us."

"Yes, but we didn't get a brainstorm that marooned two old friends in this tail end of nowhere. And we can't make him swallow it when we say that it's okay, we don't mind at all."

"That's a lot to swallow, Johnny."

"What's going to happen to us, Chuck?"

"We've got ourselves a place to live and there's lots to eat. Save our ammo for the big game —a lot of eating for each bullet-and trap the smaller animals."

"I'm wondering what will happen when the flour and all the other stuff is gone. We don't have too much of it because we always figured we could bring in more."

"We'll live on meat," said Hudson. "We got bison by the million. The plains Indians lived on them alone. And in the spring, we'll find roots and in the summer berries. And in the fall, we'll harvest a half-dozen kinds of nuts."

"Some day our ammo will be gone, no matter how careful we are with it."

"Bows and arrows. Slingshots. Spears."

"There's a lot of beasts here I wouldn't want to stand up to with nothing but a spear."

"We won't stand up to them. We'll duck when we can and run when we can't duck. Without our guns, we're no lords of creation-not in this place. If we're going to live, we'll have to recognize that fact."

"And if one of us gets sick or breaks a leg or —"

"We'll do the best we can. Nobody lives forever."

But they were talking around the thing that really bothered them, Hudson told himself-each of them afraid to speak the thought aloud.

They'd live, all right, so far as food, shelter and clothing were concerned. And they'd live most of the time in plenty, for this was a fat and open-handed land and a man could make an easy living.

But the big problem-the one they were afraid to talk about-was their emptiness of purpose. To live, they had to find some meaning in a world without society.

A man cast away on a desert isle could always live for hope, but here there was no hope. A Robinson Crusoe was separated from his fellow-humans by, at the most, a few thousand miles. Here they were separated by a hundred and fifty thousand years.

Wes Adams was the lucky one so far. Even playing his thousand-to-one shot, he still held tightly to a purpose, feeble as it might be-the hope that he could repair the time machine.

We don't need to watch him now, thought Hudson. The time we'll have to watch is when he is forced to admit he can't fix the machine.

And both Hudson and Cooper had been kept sane enough, for there had been the cabin to be built and the winter's supply of wood to cut and the hunting to be done.

But then there would come a time when all the chores were finished and there was nothing left to do.

"You ready to go?" asked Cooper.

"Sure. All rested now," said Hudson.

They hoisted the pole to their shoulders and started off again.

Hudson had lain awake nights thinking of it and all the thoughts had been dead ends.

One could write a natural history of the Pleistocene, complete with photographs and sketches, and it would be a pointless thing to do, because no future scientist would ever have a chance to read it.

Or they might labor to build a memorial, a vast pyramid, perhaps, which would carry a message forward across fifteen hundred centuries, snatching with bare hands at a semblance of immortality. But if they did, they would be working against the sure and certain knowledge that it all would come to naught, for they knew in advance that no such pyramid existed in historic time.

Or they might set out to seek contemporary Man, hiking across four thousand miles of wilderness to Bering Strait and over into Asia. And having found contemporary Man cowering in his caves, they might be able to help him immeasurably along the road to his great inheritance. Except that they'd never make it and even if they did, contemporary Man undoubtedly would find some way to do them in and might eat them in the bargain.

They came out of the woods and there was the cabin, just a hundred yards away. It crouched against the hillside above the spring, with the sweep of grassland billowing beyond it to the slate-gray skyline. A trickle of smoke came up from the chimney and they saw the door was open.

"Wes oughtn't to leave it open that way," said Cooper. "No telling when a bear might decide to come visiting."

"Hey, Wes!" yelled Hudson.

But there was no sign of him.

Inside the cabin, a white sheet of paper lay on the table top. Hudson snatched it up and read it, with Cooper at his shoulder.

> Dear guys —I don't want to get your hopes up again and have you disappointed. But I think I may have found the trouble. I'm going to try it out. If it doesn't work, I'll come back and burn this note and never say a word. But if you find the note, you'll know it worked and I'll be back to get you. Wes.

Hudson crumpled the note in his hand. "The crazy fool!"

"He's gone off his rocker," Cooper said. "He just thought...."

The same thought struck them both and they bolted for the door. At the corner of the cabin, they skidded to a halt and stood there, staring at the ridge above them.

The pyramid of rocks they'd built two months ago was gone!

CHAPTER XI

The crash brought Gen. Leslie Bowers (ret.) up out of bed-about two feet out of bed-old muscles tense, white mustache bristling.

Even at his age, the general was a man of action. He flipped the covers back, swung his feet out to the floor and grabbed the shotgun leaning against the wall.

Muttering, he blundered out of the bedroom, marched across the dining room and charged into the kitchen. There, beside the door, he snapped on the switch that turned on the floodlights. He practically took the door off its hinges getting to the stoop and he stood there, bare feet gripping the planks, nightshirt billowing in the wind, the shotgun poised and ready.

"What's going on out there?" he bellowed.

There was a tremendous pile of rocks resting where he'd parked his car. One crumpled fender and a drunken headlight peeped out of the rubble.

A man was clambering carefully down the jumbled stones, making a detour to dodge the battered fender.

The general pulled back the hammer of the gun and fought to control himself.

The man reached the bottom of the pile and turned around to face him. The general saw that he was hugging something tightly to his chest.

"Mister," the general told him, "your explanation better be a good one. That was a brand-new car. And this was the first time I was set for a night of sleep since my tooth quit aching."

The man just stood and looked at him.

"Who in thunder are you?" roared the general.

The man walked slowly forward. He stopped at the bottom of the stoop.

"My name is Wesley Adams," he said. "I'm —"

"Wesley Adams!" howled the general. "My God, man, where have you been all these years?"

"Well, I don't imagine you'll believe me, but the fact is...."

"We've been waiting for you. For twenty-five long years! Or, rather, *I've* been waiting for you. Those other idiots gave up. I've waited right here for you, Adams, for the last three years, ever since they called off the guard."

Adams gulped. "I'm sorry about the car. You see, it was this way...."

The general, he saw, was beaming at him fondly.

"I had faith in you," the general said.

He waved the shotgun by way of invitation. "Come on in. I have a call to make."

Adams stumbled up the stairs.

"Move!" the general ordered, shivering. "On the double! You want me to catch my death of cold out here?"

Inside, he fumbled for the lights and turned them on. He laid the shotgun across the kitchen table and picked up the telephone.

"Give me the White House at Washington," he said. "Yes, I said the White House.... The President? Naturally he's the one I want to talk to.... Yes, it's all right. He won't mind my calling him."

"Sir," said Adams tentatively.

The general looked up. "What is it, Adams? Go ahead and say it."

"Did you say *twenty-five* years?"

"That's what I said. What were you doing all that time?"

Adams grasped the table and hung on. "But it wasn't...."

"Yes," said the general to the operator. "Yes, I'll wait."

He held his hand over the receiver and looked inquiringly at Adams. "I imagine you'll want the same terms as before."

"Terms?"

"Sure. Recognition. Point Four Aid. Defense pact."

"I suppose so," Adams said.

"You got these saps across the barrel," the general told him happily. "You can get anything you want. You rate it, too, after what you've done and the bonehead treatment you got-but especially for not selling out."

CHAPTER XII

The night editor read the bulletin just off the teletype.

"Well, what do you know!" he said. "We just recognized Mastodonia."

He looked at the copy chief.

"Where the hell is Mastodonia?" he asked.

The copy chief shrugged. "Don't ask me. You're the brains in this joint."

"Well, let's get a map for the next edition," said the night editor.

CHAPTER XIII

Tabby, the saber-tooth, dabbed playfully at Cooper with his mighty paw.

Cooper kicked him in the ribs-an equally playful gesture.

Tabby snarled at him.

"Show your teeth at me, will you!" said Cooper. "Raised you from a kitten and that's the gratitude you show. Do it just once more and I'll belt you in the chops."

Tabby lay down blissfully and began to wash his face.

"Some day," warned Hudson, "that cat will miss a meal and that's the day you're it."

"Gentle as a dove," Cooper assured him. "Wouldn't hurt a fly."

"Well, one thing about it, nothing dares to bother us with that monstrosity around."

"Best watchdog there ever was. Got to have something to guard all this stuff we've got. When Wes gets back, we'll be millionaires. All those furs and ginseng and the ivory."

"*If* he gets back."

"He'll be back. Quit your worrying."

"But it's been five years," Hudson protested.

"He'll be back. Something happened, that's all. He's probably working on it right now. Could be that he messed up the time setting when he repaired the unit or it might have been knocked out of kilter when Buster hit the helicopter. That would take a while to fix. I don't worry that he won't come back. What I can't figure out is why did he go and leave us?"

"I've told you," Hudson said. "He was afraid it wouldn't work."

"There wasn't any need to be scared of that. We never would have laughed at him."

"No. Of course we wouldn't."

"Then what *was* he scared of?" Cooper asked.

"If the unit failed and we knew it failed, Wes was afraid we'd try to make him see how hopeless and insane it was. And he knew we'd probably convince him and then all his hope would be gone. And he wanted to hang onto that, Johnny. He wanted to hang onto his hope even when there wasn't any left."

"That doesn't matter now," said Cooper. "What counts is that he'll come back. I can feel it in my bones."

And here's another case, thought Hudson, of hope begging to be allowed to go on living.

God, he thought, I wish I could be that blind!

"Wes is working on it right now," said Cooper confidently.

CHAPTER XIV

He was. Not he alone, but a thousand others, working desperately, knowing that the time was short, working not alone for two men trapped in time, but for the peace they all had dreamed about-that the whole world had yearned for through the ages.

For to be of any use, it was imperative that they could zero in the time machines they meant to build as an artilleryman would zero in a battery of guns, that each time machine would take its occupants to the same instant of the past, that their operation would extend over the same period of time, to the exact second.

It was a problem of control and calibration-starting with a prototype that was calibrated, as its finest adjustment, for jumps of 50,000 years.

Project Mastodon was finally under way.

Second Childhood

> Achieving immortality is only half of the problem.
> The other half is knowing how to live with it once
> it's been made possible-and inescapable!

You did not die.

There was no normal way to die.

You lived as carelessly and as recklessly as you could and you hoped that you would be lucky and be accidentally killed.

You kept on living and you got tired of living.

"God, how tired a man can get of living!" Andrew Young said.

John Riggs, chairman of the immortality commission, cleared his throat.

"You realize," he said to Andrew Young, "that this petition is a highly irregular procedure to bring to our attention."

He picked up the sheaf of papers off the table and ruffled through them rapidly.

"There is no precedent," he added.

"I had hoped," said Andrew Young, "to establish precedent."

Commissioner Stanford said, "I must admit that you have made a good case, Ancestor Young. Yet you must realize that this commission has no possible jurisdiction over the life of any person, except to see that everyone is assured of all the benefits of immortality and to work out any kinks that may show up."

"I am well aware of that," answered Young, "and it seems to me that my case is one of the kinks you mention."

He stood silently, watching the faces of the members of the board. They are afraid, he thought. Every one of them. Afraid of the day they will face the thing I am facing now. They have sought an answer and there is no answer yet except the pitifully basic answer, the brutally fundamental answer that I have given them.

"My request is simple," he told them, calmly. "I have asked for permission to discontinue life. And since suicide has been made psychologically impossible, I have asked that this commission appoint a panel of next-friends to make the necessary and somewhat distasteful arrangements to bring about the discontinuance of my life."

"If we did," said Riggs, "we would destroy everything we have. There is no virtue in a life of only five thousand years. No more than in a life of only a hundred years. If Man is to be immortal, he must be genuinely immortal. He cannot compromise."

"And yet," said Young, "my friends are gone."

* * * * *

He gestured at the papers Riggs held in his hands. "I have them listed there," he said. "Their names and when and where and how they died. Take a look at them. More than two hundred names. People of my own generation and of the generations closely following mine. Their names and the photo-copies of their death certificates."

He put both of his hands upon the table, palms flat against the table, and leaned his weight upon his arms.

"Take a look at how they died," he said. "Every one involves accidental violence. Some of them drove their vehicles too fast and, more than likely, very recklessly. One fell off a cliff when he reached down to pick a flower that was growing on its edge. A case of deliberately poor judgment, to my mind. One got stinking drunk and took a bath and passed out in the tub. He drowned...."

"Ancestor Young," Riggs said sharply, "you are surely not implying these folks were suicides."

"No," Andrew Young said bitterly. "We abolished suicide three thousand years ago, cleared it clean out of human minds. How could they have killed themselves?"

Stanford said, peering up at Young, "I believe, sir, you sat on the board that resolved that problem."

Andrew Young nodded. "It was after the first wave of suicides. I remember it quite well. It took years of work. We had to change human perspective, shift certain facets of human nature. We had to condition human reasoning by education and propaganda and instill a new set of moral values. I think we did a good job of it. Perhaps too good a job. Today a man can no more think of deliberately committing suicide than he could think of overthrowing our government. The very idea, the very word is repulsive, instinctively repulsive. You can come a long way, gentlemen, in three thousand years."

He leaned across the table and tapped the sheaf of papers with a lean, tense finger.

"They didn't kill themselves," he said. "They did not commit suicide. They just didn't give a damn. They were tired of living ... as I am tired of living. So they lived recklessly in every way. Perhaps there always was a secret hope that they would drown while drunk or their car would hit a tree or...."

* * * * *

He straightened up and faced them. "Gentlemen," he said. "I am 5,786 years of age. I was born at Lancaster, Maine, on the planet Earth on September 21, 1968. I have served humankind well in those fifty-seven centuries. My record is there for you to see. Boards, commissions, legislative posts, diplomatic missions. No one can say that I have shirked my duty. I submit that I have paid any debt I owe humanity ... even the well-intentioned debt for a chance at immortality."

"We wish," said Riggs, "that you would reconsider."

"I am a lonely man," replied Young. "A lonely man and tired. I have no friends. There is nothing any longer that holds my interest. It is my hope that I can make you see the desirability of assuming jurisdiction in cases such as mine. Someday you may find a solution to the problem, but until that time arrives, I ask you, in the name of mercy, to give us relief from life."

"The problem, as we see it," said Riggs, "is to find some way to wipe out mental perspective. When a man lives as you have, sir, for fifty centuries, he has too long a memory. The memories add up to the disadvantage of present realities and prospects for the future."

"I know," said Young. "I remember we used to talk about that in the early days. It was one of the problems which was recognized when immortality first became practical. But we always thought that memory would erase itself, that the brain could accommodate only so many memories, that when it got full up it would dump the old ones. It hasn't worked that way."

He made a savage gesture. "Gentlemen, I can recall my childhood much more vividly than I recall anything that happened yesterday."

"Memories are buried," said Riggs, "and in the old days, when men lived no longer than a hundred years at most, it was thought those buried memories were forgotten. Life, Man told himself, is a process of forgetting. So Man wasn't too worried over memories when he became immortal. He thought he would forget them."

"He should have known," argued Young. "I can remember my father, and I remember him much more intimately than I will remember you gentlemen once I leave this room.... I can remember my father telling me that, in his later years, he could recall things which happened in his childhood that had been forgotten all his younger years. And that, alone, should have tipped us off. The brain buries only the newer memories deeply ... they are not available; they do not rise to bother one, because they are not sorted or oriented or correlated or whatever it is that the brain may do with them. But once they are all nicely docketed and filed, they pop up in an instant."

* * * * *

Riggs nodded agreement. "There's a lag of a good many years in the brain's bookkeeping. We will overcome it in time."

"We have tried," said Stanford. "We tried conditioning, the same solution that worked with suicides. But in this, it didn't work. For a man's life is built upon his memories. There are certain basic memories that must remain intact. With conditioning, you could not be selective. You could not keep the structural memories and winnow out the trash. It didn't work that way."

"There was one machine that worked," Riggs put in. "It got rid of memories. I don't understand exactly how it worked, but it did the job all right. It did too good a job. It swept the mind as clean as an empty room. It didn't leave a thing. It took all memories and it left no capacity to build a new set. A man went in a human being and came out a vegetable."

"Suspended animation," said Stanford, "would be a solution. If we had suspended animation. Simply stack a man away until we found the answer, then revive and recondition him."

"Be that as it may," Young told them, "I should like your most earnest consideration of my petition. I do not feel quite equal to waiting until you have the answer solved."

Riggs said, harshly, "You are asking us to legalize death."

Young nodded. "If you wish to phrase it that way. I'm asking it in the name of common decency."

Commissioner Stanford said, "We can ill afford to lose you, Ancestor."

Young sighed. "There is that damned attitude again. Immortality pays all debts. When a man is made immortal, he has received full compensation for everything that he may endure. I have lived longer than any man could be expected to live and still I am denied the dignity of old age. A man's desires are few, and quickly sated, and yet he is expected to continue living with desires burned up and blown away to ash. He gets to a point where nothing has a value ... even to a point where his own personal values are no more than shadows. Gentlemen, there was a time when I could not have committed murder ... literally could not have forced myself to kill another man ... but today I could, without a second thought. Disillusion and cynicism have crept in upon me and I have no conscience."

* * * * *

"There are compensations," Riggs said. "Your family...."

"They get in my hair," said Young disgustedly. "Thousands upon thousands of young squirts calling me Grandsire and Ancestor and coming to me for advice they practically never follow. I don't know even a fraction of them and I listen to them carefully explain a relationship so tangled and trivial that it makes me yawn in their faces. It's all new to them and so old, so damned and damnably old to me."

"Ancestor Young," said Stanford, "you have seen Man spread out from Earth to distant stellar systems. You have seen the human race expand from one planet to several thousand planets. You have had a part in this. Is there not some satisfaction...."

"You're talking in abstracts," Young cut in. "What I am concerned about is myself ... a certain specific mass of protoplasm shaped in biped form and tagged by the designation, ironic as it may seem, of Andrew Young. I have been unselfish all my life. I've asked little for myself. Now I am being utterly and entirely selfish and I ask that this matter be regarded as a personal problem rather than as a racial abstraction."

"Whether you'll admit it or not," said Stanford, "it is more than a personal problem. It is a problem which some day must be solved for the salvation of the race."

"That is what I am trying to impress upon you," Young snapped. "It is a problem that you must face. Some day you will solve it, but until you do, you must make provisions for those who face the unsolved problem."

"Wait a while," counseled Chairman Riggs. "Who knows? Today, tomorrow."

"Or a million years from now," Young told him bitterly and left, a tall, vigorous-looking man whose step was swift in anger where normally it was slow with weariness and despair.

* * * * *

There was yet a chance, of course.

But there was little hope.

How can a man go back almost six thousand years and snare a thing he never understood?

And yet Andrew Young remembered it. Remembered it as clearly as if it had been a thing that had happened in the morning of this very day.

It was a shining thing, a bright thing, a happiness that was brand-new and fresh as a bluebird's wing of an April morning or a shy woods flower after sudden rain.

He had been a boy and he had seen the bluebird and he had no words to say the thing he felt, but he had held up his tiny fingers and pointed and shaped his lips to coo.

Once, he thought, I had it in my very fingers and I did not have the experience to know what it was, nor the value of it. And now I know the value, but it has escaped me-it escaped me on the day that I began to think like a human being. The first adult thought pushed it just a little and the next one pushed it farther and finally it was gone entirely and I didn't even know that it had gone.

He sat in the chair on the flagstone patio and felt the Sun upon him, filtering through the branches of trees misty with the breaking leaves of Spring.

Something else, thought Andrew Young. Something that was not human-yet. A tiny animal that had many ways to choose, many roads to walk. And, of course, I chose the wrong way. I chose the human way. But there was another way. I know there must have been. A fairy way-or a brownie way, or maybe even pixie. That sounds foolish and childish now, but it wasn't always.

I chose the human way because I was guided into it. I was pushed and shoved, like a herded sheep.

I grew up and I lost the thing I held.

He sat and made his mind go hard and tried to analyze what it was he sought and there was no name for it. Except happiness. And happiness was a state of being, not a thing to regain and grasp.

* * * * *

But he could remember how it felt. With his eyes open in the present, he could remember the brightness of the day of the past, the clean-washed goodness of it, the wonder of the colors that were more brilliant than he ever since had seen-as if it were the first second after Creation and the world was still shiningly new.

It was that new, of course. It would be that new to a child.

But that didn't explain it all.

It didn't explain the bottomless capacity for seeing and knowing and believing in the beauty and the goodness of a clean new world. It didn't explain the almost non-human elation of knowing that there were colors to see and scents to smell and soft green grass to touch.

I'm insane, Andrew Young said to himself. Insane, or going insane. But if insanity will take me back to an understanding of the strange perception I had when I was a child, and lost, I'll take insanity.

He leaned back in his chair and let his eyes go shut and his mind drift back.

He was crouching in a corner of a garden and the leaves were drifting down from the walnut trees like a rain of saffron gold. He lifted one of the leaves and it slipped from his fingers, for his hands were chubby still and not too sure in grasping. But he tried again and he clutched it by the stem in one stubby fist and he saw that it was not just a blob of yellowness, but delicate, with many little veins. When he held it so that the Sun struck it, he imagined that he could almost see through it, the gold was spun so fine.

He crouched with the leaf clutched tightly in his hand and for a moment there was a silence that held him motionless. Then he heard the frost-loosened leaves pattering all around him, pattering as they fell, talking in little whispers as they sailed down through the air and found themselves a bed with their golden fellows.

In that moment he knew that he was one with the leaves and the whispers that they made, one with the gold and the autumn sunshine and the far blue mist upon the hill above the apple orchard.

A foot crunched stone behind him and his eyes came open and the golden leaves were gone.

"I am sorry if I disturbed you, Ancestor," said the man. "I had an appointment for this hour, but I would not have disturbed you if I had known."

Young stared at him reproachfully without answering.

"I am kin," the man told him.

"I wouldn't doubt it," said Andrew Young. "The Galaxy is cluttered up with descendants of mine."

The man was very humble. "Of course, you must resent us sometimes. But we are proud of you, sir. I might almost say that we revere you. No other family —"

"I know," interrupted Andrew Young. "No other family has any fossil quite so old as I am."

"Nor as wise," said the man.

Andrew Young snorted. "Cut out that nonsense. Let's hear what you have to say and get it over with."

* * * * *

The technician was harassed and worried and very frankly puzzled. But he stayed respectful, for one always was respectful to an ancestor, whoever he might be. Today there were mighty few left who had been born into a mortal world.

Not that Andrew Young looked old. He looked like all adults, a fine figure of a person in the early twenties.

The technician shifted uneasily. "But, sir, this ... this...."

"Teddy bear," said Young.

"Yes, of course. An extinct terrestrial subspecies of animal?"

"It's a toy," Young told him. "A very ancient toy. All children used to have them five thousand years ago. They took them to bed."

* * * * *

The technician shuddered. "A deplorable custom. Primitive."

"Depends on the viewpoint," said Young. "I've slept with them many a time. There's a world of comfort in one, I can personally assure you."

The technician saw that it was no use to argue. He might as well fabricate the thing and get it over with.

"I can build you a fine model, sir," he said, trying to work up some enthusiasm. "I'll build in a response mechanism so that it can give simple answers to certain keyed questions and, of course, I'll fix it so it'll walk, either on two legs or four...."

"No," said Andrew Young.

The technician looked surprised and hurt. "No?"

"No," repeated Andrew Young. "I don't want it fancied up. I want it a simple lump of make-believe. No wonder the children of today have no imagination. Modern toys entertain them with a bag of tricks that leave the young'uns no room for imagination. They couldn't possibly think up, on their own, all the screwy things these new toys do. Built-in responses and implied consciousness and all such mechanical trivia...."

"You just want a stuffed fabric," said the technician, sadly, "with jointed arms and legs."

"Precisely," agreed Young.

"You're sure you want fabric, sir? I could do a neater job in plastics."

"Fabric," Young insisted firmly, "and it must be scratchy."

"Scratchy, sir?"

"Sure. You know. Bristly. So it scratches when you rub your face against it."

"But no one in his right mind would want to rub his face...."

"I would," said Andrew Young. "I fully intend to do so."

"As you wish, sir," the technician answered, beaten now.

"When you get it done," said Young, "I have some other things in mind."

"Other things?" The technician looked wildly about, as if seeking some escape.

"A high chair," said Young. "And a crib. And a woolly dog. And buttons."

"Buttons?" asked the technician. "What are buttons?"

"I'll explain it all to you," Young told him airily. "It all is very simple."

* * * * *

It seemed, when Andrew Young came into the room, that Riggs and Stanford had been expecting him, had known that he was coming and had been waiting for him.

He wasted no time on preliminaries or formalities.

They know, he told himself. They know, or they have guessed. They would be watching me. Ever since I brought in my petition, they have been watching me, wondering what I would be thinking, trying to puzzle out what I might do next. They know every move I've made, they know about the toys and the furniture and all the other things. And I don't need to tell them what I plan to do.

"I need some help," he said, and they nodded soberly, as if they had guessed he needed help.

"I want to build a house," he explained. "A big house. Much larger than the usual house."

Riggs said, "We'll draw the plans for you. Do anything else that you —"

"A house," Young went on, "about four or five times as big as the ordinary house. Four or five times normal scale, I mean. Doors twenty-five to thirty feet high and everything else in proportion."

"Neighbors or privacy?" asked Stanford.

"Privacy," said Young.

"We'll take care of it," promised Riggs. "Leave the matter of the house to us."

Young stood for a long moment, looking at the two of them. Then he said, "I thank you, gentlemen. I thank you for your helpfulness and your understanding. But most of all I thank you for not asking any questions."

He turned slowly and walked out of the room and they sat in silence for minutes after he was gone.

Finally, Stanford offered a deduction: "It will have to be a place that a boy would like. Woods to run in and a little stream to fish in and a field where he can fly his kites. What else could it be?"

"He's been out ordering children's furniture and toys," Riggs agreed. "Stuff from five thousand years ago. The kind of things he used when he was a child. But scaled to adult size."

"Now," said Stanford, "he wants a house built to the same proportions. A house that will make him think or help him believe that he is a child. But will it work, Riggs? His body will not change. He cannot make it change. It will only be in his mind."

"Illusion," declared Riggs. "The illusion of bigness in relation to himself. To a child, creeping on the floor, a door is twenty-five to thirty feet high, relatively. Of course the child doesn't know that. But Andrew Young does. I don't see how he'll overcome that."

"At first," suggested Stanford, "he will know that it's illusion, but after a time, isn't there a possibility that it will become reality so far as he's concerned? That's why he needs our help. So that the house will not be firmly planted in his memory as a thing that's merely out of proportion ... so that it will slide from illusion into reality without too great a strain."

"We must keep our mouths shut." Riggs nodded soberly. "There must be no interference. It's a thing he must do himself ... entirely by himself. Our help with the house must be the help of an unseen, silent agency. Like brownies, I think the term was that he used, we must help and be never seen. Intrusion by anyone would introduce a jarring note and would destroy illusion and that is all he has to work on. Illusion pure and simple."

"Others have tried," objected Stanford, pessimistic again. "Many others. With gadgets and machines...."

"None has tried it," said Riggs, "with the power of mind alone. With the sheer determination to wipe out five thousand years of memory."

"That will be his stumbling block," said Stanford. "The old, dead memories are the things he has to beat. He has to get rid of them ... not just bury them, but get rid of them for good and all, forever."

"He must do more than that," said Riggs. "He must replace his memories with the outlook he had when he was a child. His mind must be washed out, refreshed, wiped clean and shining and made new again ... ready to live another five thousand years."

The two men sat and looked at one another and in each other's eyes they saw a single thought—the day would come when they, too, each of them alone, would face the problem Andrew Young faced.

"We must help," said Riggs, "in every way we can and we must keep watch and we must be ready ... but Andrew Young cannot know that we are helping or that we are watching him. We must anticipate the materials and tools and the aids that he may need."

* * * * *

Stanford started to speak, then hesitated, as if seeking in his mind for the proper words.

"Yes," said Riggs. "What is it?"

"Later on," Stanford managed to say, "much later on, toward the very end, there is a certain factor that we must supply. The one thing that he will need the most and the one thing that he cannot think about, even in advance. All the rest can be stage setting and he can still go on toward the time when it becomes reality. All the rest may be make-believe, but one thing must come as genuine or the entire effort will collapse in failure."

Riggs nodded. "Of course. That's something we'll have to work out carefully."

"If we can," Stanford said.

* * * * *

The yellow button over here and the red one over there and the green one doesn't fit, so I'll throw it on the floor and just for the fun of it, I'll put the pink one in my mouth and someone will find me with it and they'll raise a ruckus because they will be afraid that I will swallow it.

And there's nothing, absolutely nothing, that I love better than a full-blown ruckus. Especially if it is over me.

"Ug," said Andrew Young, and he swallowed the button.

He sat stiff and straight in the towering high chair and then, in a fury, swept the oversized muffin tin and its freight of buttons crashing to the floor.

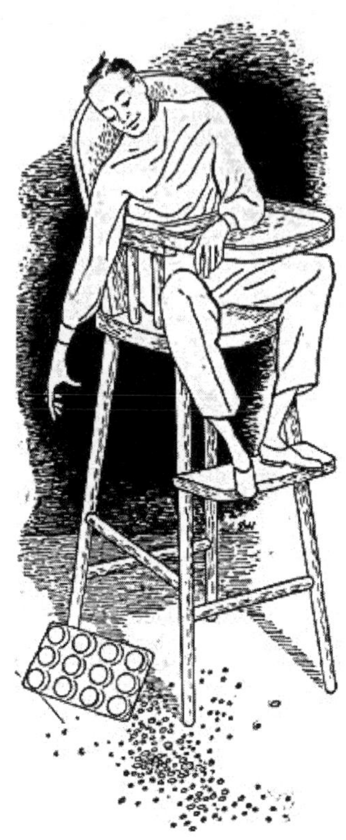

For a second he felt like weeping in utter frustration and then a sense of shame crept in on him.

Big baby, he said to himself.

Crazy to be sitting in an overgrown high chair, playing with buttons and mouthing baby talk and trying to force a mind conditioned by five thousand years of life into the channels of an infant's thoughts.

Carefully he disengaged the tray and slid it out, cautiously shinnied down the twelve-foot-high chair.

The room engulfed him, the ceiling towering far above him.

The neighbors, he told himself, no doubt thought him crazy, although none of them had said so. Come to think of it, he had not seen any of his neighbors for a long spell now.

A suspicion came into his mind. Maybe they knew what he was doing, maybe they were deliberately keeping out of his way in order not to embarrass him.

That, of course, would be what they would do if they had realized what he was about. But he had expected ... he had expected ... that fellow, what's his name? ... at the commission, what's the name of that commission, anyhow? Well, anyway, he'd expected a fellow whose name he couldn't remember from a commission the name of which he could not recall to come snooping around, wondering what he might be up to, offering to help, spoiling the whole setup, everything he'd planned.

I can't remember, he complained to himself. I can't remember the name of a man whose name I knew so short a time ago as yesterday. Nor the name of a commission that I knew as well as I know my name. I'm getting forgetful. I'm getting downright childish.

Childish?

Childish!

Childish and forgetful.

Good Lord, thought Andrew Young, that's just the way I want it.

On hands and knees he scrabbled about and picked up the buttons, put them in his pocket. Then, with the muffin tin underneath his arm, he shinnied up the high chair and, seating himself comfortably, sorted out the buttons in the pan.

The green one over here in this compartment and the yellow one … oops, there she goes onto the floor. And the red one in with the blue one and this one … this one … what's the color of this one? Color? What's that?

What is what?

What —

* * * * *

"It's almost time," said Stanford, "and we are ready, as ready as we'll ever be. We'll move in when the time is right, but we can't move in too soon. Better to be a little late than a little early. We have all the things we need. Special size diapers and —"

"Good Lord," exclaimed Riggs, "it won't go that far, will it?"

"It should," said Stanford. "It should go even further to work right. He got lost yesterday. One of our men found him and led him home. He didn't have the slightest idea where he was and he was getting pretty scared and he cried a little. He chattered about birds and flowers and he insisted that our man stay and play with him."

Riggs chuckled softly. "Did he?"

"Oh, certainly. He came back worn to a frazzle."

"Food?" I asked Riggs. "How is he feeding himself?"

"We see there's a supply of stuff, cookies and such-wise, left on a low shelf, where he can get at them. One of the robots cooks up some more substantial stuff on a regular schedule and leaves it where he can find it. We have to be careful. We can't mess around too much. We can't intrude on him. I have a feeling he's almost reached an actual turning point. We can't afford to upset things now that he's come this far."

"The android's ready?"

"Just about," said Stanford.

"And the playmates?"

"Ready. They were less of a problem."

"There's nothing more that we can do?"

"Nothing," Stanford said. "Just wait, that's all. Young has carried himself this far by the sheer force of will alone. That will is gone now. He can't consciously force himself any further back. He is more child than adult now. He's built up a regressive momentum and the only question is whether that momentum is sufficient to carry him all the way back to actual babyhood."

"It has to go back to that?" Riggs looked unhappy, obviously thinking of his own future. "You're only guessing, aren't you?"

"All the way or it simply is no good," Stanford said dogmatically. "He has to get an absolutely fresh start. All the way or nothing."

"And if he gets stuck halfway between? Half child, half man, what then?"

"That's something I don't want to think about," Stanford said.

* * * * *

He had lost his favorite teddy bear and gone to hunt it in the dusk that was filled with elusive fireflies and the hush of a world quieting down for the time of sleep. The grass was drenched with dew and he felt the cold wetness of it soaking through his shoes as he went from bush to hedge to flowerbed, looking for the missing toy.

It was necessary, he told himself, that he find the nice little bear, for it was the one that slept with him and if he did not find it, he knew that it would spend a lonely and comfortless night. But at no time did he admit, even to his innermost thought, that it was he who needed the bear and not the bear who needed him.

A soaring bat swooped low and for a horrified moment, catching sight of the zooming terror, a blob of darkness in the gathering dusk, he squatted low against the ground, huddling against the sudden fear that came out of the night. Sounds of fright bubbled in his throat and now he saw the great dark garden as an unknown place, filled with lurking shadows that lay in wait for him.

He stayed cowering against the ground and tried to fight off the alien fear that growled from behind each bush and snarled in every darkened corner. But even as the fear washed over him, there was one hidden corner of his mind that knew there was no need of fear. It was as if that one area of his brain still fought against the rest of him, as if that small section of cells might know that the bat was no more than a flying bat, that the shadows in the garden were no more than absence of light.

There was a reason, he knew, why he should not be afraid —a good reason born of a certain knowledge he no longer had. And that he should have such knowledge seemed unbelievable, for he was scarcely two years old.

* * * * *

He tried to say it-two years old.

There was something wrong with his tongue, something the matter with the way he had to use his mouth, with the way his lips refused to shape the words he meant to say.

He tried to define the words, tried to tell himself what he meant by two years old and one moment it seemed that he knew the meaning of it and then it escaped him.

The bat came again and he huddled close against the ground, shivering as he crouched. He lifted his eyes fearfully, darting glances here and there, and out of the corner of his eye he saw the looming house and it was a place he knew as refuge.

"House," he said, and the word was wrong, not the word itself, but the way he said it.

He ran on trembling, unsure feet and the great door loomed before him, with the latch too high to reach. But there was another way, a small swinging door built into the big door, the sort of door that is built for cats and dogs and sometimes little children. He darted through it and felt the sureness and the comfort of the house about him. The sureness and the comfort-and the loneliness.

He found his second-best teddy bear, and, picking it up, clutched it to his breast, sobbing into its scratchy back in pure relief from terror.

There is something wrong, he thought. Something dreadfully wrong. Something is as it should not be. It is not the garden or the darkened bushes or the swooping winged shape that came out of the night. It is something else, something missing, something that should be here and isn't.

Clutching the teddy bear, he sat rigid and tried desperately to drive his mind back along the way that would tell him what was wrong. There was an answer, he was sure of that. There was an answer somewhere; at one time he had known it. At one time he had recognized the need he felt and there had been no way to supply it-and now he couldn't even know the need, could feel it, but he could not know it.

He clutched the bear closer and huddled in the darkness, watching the moonbeam that came through a window, high above his head, and etched a square of floor in brightness.

Fascinated, he watched the moonbeam and all at once the terror faded. He dropped the bear and crawled on hands and knees, stalking the moonbeam. It did not try to get away and he reached its edge and thrust his hands into it and laughed with glee when his hands were painted by the light coming through the window.

He lifted his face and stared up at the blackness and saw the white globe of the Moon, looking at him, watching him. The Moon seemed to wink at him and he chortled joyfully.

Behind him a door creaked open and he turned clumsily around.

Someone stood in the doorway, almost filling it —a beautiful person who smiled at him. Even in the darkness he could sense the sweetness of the smile, the glory of her golden hair.

"Time to eat, Andy," said the woman. "Eat and get a bath and then to bed."

Andrew Young hopped joyfully on both feet, arms held out-happy and excited and contented. "Mummy!" he cried. "Mummy ... Moon!"

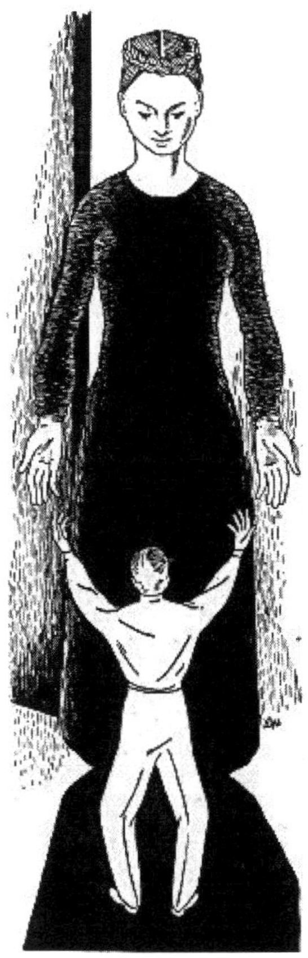

He swung about with a pointing finger and the woman came swiftly across the floor, knelt and put her arms around him, held him close against her. His cheek against hers, he stared up at the Moon and it was a wondrous thing, a bright and golden thing, a wonder that was shining new and fresh.

* * * * *

On the street outside, Stanford and Riggs stood looking up at the huge house that towered above the trees.

"She's in there now," said Stanford. "Everything's quiet so it must be all right."

Riggs said, "He was crying in the garden. He ran in terror for the house. He stopped crying about the time she must have come in."

Stanford nodded. "I was afraid we were putting it off too long, but I don't see now how we could have done it sooner. Any outside interference would have shattered the thing he tried to do. He had to really need her. Well, it's all right now. The timing was just about perfect."

"You're sure, Stanford?"

"Sure? Certainly I am sure. We created the android and we trained her. We instilled a deep maternal sense into her personality. She knows what to do. She is almost human. She is as close as we could come to a human mother eighteen feet tall. We don't know what Young's mother looked like, but chances are he doesn't either. Over the years his memory has idealized her. That's what we did. We made an ideal mother."

"If it only works," said Riggs.

"It will work," said Stanford, confidently. "Despite the shortcomings we may discover by trial and error, it will work. He's been fighting himself all this time. Now he can quit fighting and shift responsibility. It's enough to get him over the final hump, to place him safely and securely in the second childhood that he had to have. Now he can curl up, contented. There is someone to look after him and think for him and take care of him. He'll probably go back just a little further ... a little closer to the cradle. And that is good, for the further he goes, the more memories are erased."

"And then?" asked Riggs worriedly.

"Then he can proceed to grow up again."

They stood watching, silently.

In the enormous house, lights came on in the kitchen and the windows gleamed with a homey brightness.

I, too, Stanford was thinking. Some day, I, too. Young has pointed the way, he has blazed the path. He had shown us, all the other billions of us, here on Earth and all over the Galaxy, the way it can be done. There will be others and for them there will be more help. We'll know then how to do it better.

Now we have something to work on.

Another thousand years or so, he thought, and I will go back, too. Back to the cradle and the dreams of childhood and the safe security of a mother's arms.

It didn't frighten him in the least.